GAMES MASTER
PRESENTS

STAY ALIVE
IN MINECRAFT

SCHOLASTIC INC.

EDITORIAL DIRECTOR
Jon White

EDITOR
Amy Best

WRITERS
Wesley Copeland, Emma Davies, Jamie Frier,
Joel McIver, Dom Reseigh-Lincoln

CONTRIBUTOR
Luke Albigés

LEAD DESIGNER
Adam Markiewicz

DESIGNERS
Andy Downes, Madelene King, Laurie Newman

PRODUCTION
Sarah Bankes, Dan Peel

ISBN: 978-1-338-32531-7

10 9 8 7 6 5 4 3 2   18 19 20 21 22

Printed in the U.S.A.   40
First edition, November 2018

WELCOME TO
STAY ALIVE
IN MINECRAFT

Minecraft is a worldwide sensation, with people all over the globe picking up their controllers and tapping away at their keys to immerse themselves in its vast world. However, Minecraft goes beyond building cool structures. You'll encounter many friendly faces, but also some not-so-friendly ones too. With this essential guide, we will show you how to defend yourself against your enemies and stay alive for as long as possible, whether that be by building the ultimate fortress, or by simply knowing your enemy. Look inside for the best tips and tricks to help you become the ultimate survivor.

Contents

06

38

108

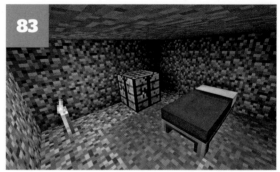

83

116

THE HIGH-WALL FORTRESS

How to build an epic fort to keep your enemies at bay

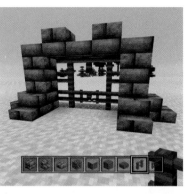

01
FIND SOME SPACE

Start by finding yourself a big ol' open space — you'll need it! Then add stone bricks, stone steps, spruce wood, and a spruce-wood fence to your hotbar. Next create a three-wide doorframe from the stone bricks and lay down steps in front to act as pillars. Make a five-long wall on both sides of the door, then add spruce wood at both ends. Add some more pillars at the base of the spruce, before using steps to design the windows.

02
THE OTHER WALLS

Run a layer of spruce half-slabs on top of the wall. Next up, lay stone half-slabs and stone bricks along the top, one block out to create a battlement formation. Now create three more walls, this time by counting 13 blocks out, dropping down spruce wood so you know where the corners will be. From there, add in the pillars at the base of the spruce, then continue the castle formation all around the newest three sides.

Who doesn't love building castles of epic proportions? Everyone loves building forts. That's a Minecraft fact. Just like how everyone gets jump-scared by sneaky Creepers at some point in Survival. In this guide, we'll be showing you how to make a killer fort, how to design walls and avoid making a square fort, as well as showing off some nifty lookout post designs that anyone can build. For this build, we'll be using the Skyrim texture pack. If you don't own the Skyrim mash-up, never fear — the Fantasy pack or even the base game pack can still yield glorious results.

03
FINISHING THE WALLS

What we'll be doing next is essentially copying the front face, only on the other three sides. With the other corners in place, connect the spruce half-slabs all around and back onto itself. From here, you can go ahead and use stone bricks to fill in the bulk of the walls. For the corner turrets, just lay down extra stone half-slabs so they tower over the smaller stone spikes.

△ Inventory   ☐ Creative

04
THE TOP SECTION

With the spruce half-slabs around the outside, grab some stone half-slabs and run them around the inside in a clockwork fashion. The reason for this is that if you run it around the inside like this, you should end up with a five-by-five gap in the middle. In this gap, create a small room with castle turrets on top, then mine the corners out and replace with spruce wood. You've now got yourself a neat little room on top.

△ Inventory   ☐ Creative

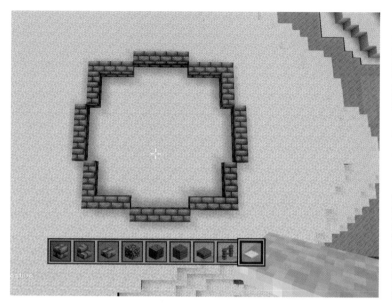

05
THE NEXT LOOKOUT

Around 30 blocks away from the left of the mini-fort is where we'll be building our next section. Don't worry about being exact here — just pick a nice flat space to the left that's far enough away to fit a wall between the two. Next create this weird star-like shape (five blocks for the longest sections, four for the smaller bits). Build the walls up by ten, and add fences for the windows.

06
FRONT AND SIDES

Look at the image. Are you looking? Still looking? No, you're reading this. Go look. Back now? Cool. Add in the spruce wood on the corners as shown. From here, in between the front two spruce, build up by nine blocks with spruce planks. Add in the fence on top and add in the windows every three blocks. Now build up the walls around it and add in the spruce planks and fence combo on the two sides.

07 THE FIRST ROOFS

This next part is all about building the roofs. To the right of the large wall from the last step, run stone steps in a pyramid formation angling upward. In the middle of the steps, or the corner section, use spruce steps to break up the stone a tad. Next head to the jutting out bit on the right and build it outward by three blocks. Add in spruce and fencing, then build a roof sitting nicely on top.

08 THE HIGHEST TOWER

Stretch the roof across the entire structure from one side to the other. On the back five-wide section, create a roof on top and build it back so it stops right before the roof stretching across. Now go and build two flat roofs on each of the two corner sections. You should be able to connect the two smaller sections into the roof coming from the five-wide section. Add a roof above the main tower, fill in the back wall, and this part's done!

FALLING FLOOR

Make unwanted guests fall to their dooooooooom!

1 Let's kick-start this build by digging up a wide hole. The measurements here don't matter, so make it as big or as small as you want. Just make sure you leave a four-block gap at the top, and a two-block gap below for the lava (seeing as a single layer of lava will be covered when the blocks fall).

2 With the hole all mined out, count a few blocks back, dig a hole heading straight down, then curve it into the hole. This new gap will allow us access to the underside later on, which is crucial to this build. Afterward, grab some dirt and add a layer four blocks deep into the hole. And now count the space to make sure it's definitely four blocks lower than ground level.

3 This trap uses an exploit to trick the game, so it's imperative you follow the instructions closely. Grab rosebushes and lay them on every single block of dirt. Don't use any other flowers, and make sure the rosebushes are two blocks high.

4 Lay sand on top of all the rosebushes. And to keep nosey players out, add a chest in the center. Now here comes the other important part. Follow your tunnel from Step 2 underground. First smash all the rosebushes (but not the sand or the blocks yet). Next, with all the rosebushes gone, mine up the layer of dirt.

5 Your trap is now armed and ready! The game doesn't know the blocks are floating, so when the chest opens, that updates the sand blocks and causes the ground to give way. Go ahead and cover up the hole, and if you want to change this so the trap keeps unwanted mobs away, just switch the chest for pressure plates (before you lay the sand on!).

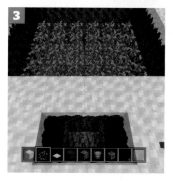

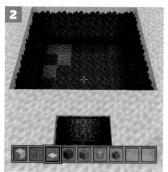

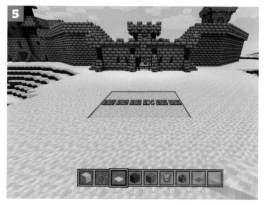

11

09 THE FINAL TOWER

Find a massive space to the right of the first structure. Here, build a two-wide door frame with inward-facing steps at the top. To the right and left of the frame, create two pillars, one block out, surrounded by steps at the top and bottom. Directly on top of the pillars, run a row of cracked stone bricks. Head back down to the doorframe and build the wall around it. Now repeat this process twice above to make a three-tiered front. With that complete, repeat the process for the other three walls.

10 TOP OF THE TOWER

For this part, we'll be laying down the groundwork for the top section. Follow the pillars up and place a single stone block in line with them on all four sides. Next drop a set of upside-down stone steps on the block facing outward. Now run a row of stone bricks on top of the steps to create a floating square. Finally add in the blocks as shown before, placing steps on top to finish off.

11 INSIDE OUT

All that's left now is to add a bit of brick work from the inside. At the top, don't forget we're inside the tower now — lay in the floor. Now pick a wall, any wall. Create the diamond shape by using a step formation heading upward toward the center, and then place actual steps on the them. When you view this from the outside, you should be left with a nice amount of both depth and texture at the top of the final tower.

12
BUILD THE WALLS UP

We're almost on the home stretch! This is the last of the real building, and all we need to do is create walls interlinking all our towers. Start by building three sets of steps coming off the right and left sides of our first structure. The wall itself is three cobblestone blocks surrounded by stone bricks. Here's a tip: Don't have straight walls or you'll end up with a square. Using straights and turns helps make it look more realistic, and that much more personal and unique.

BUILD BONUS

A MEGA BLACKSMITH FORGE

Blacksmith forges offer no useful gameplay advantages, but boy do they look great! This build, created by 04hockey in just 30 minutes, uses a mix of stone bricks, stone half-slabs, and what appears to be spruce wood and planks. The general idea here is four corner posts with four, three-wide mini-roofs on each of the different sides leading into a small tower with a light at the top so it's nice and visible from a distance. As for the continuous fire, all blocks will eventually go out with the exception of netherrack, which stays lit forever.

13
LIGHT IT UP

That's the main bulk of this build out of the way. All that's left now is to fill the inside with useful survival fodder. Why not a decent-sized house for storage? A barn for livestock? A mini-farm? A blacksmith forge? Just when you're done, don't forget to grab a load of torches and light the place up. After all, light blocks mobs from spawning. And no one wants any unexpected night visitors!

WORST WAYS TO DIE IN MINECRAFT

"O death, where is thy sting?" Getting killed in Minecraft can be embarrassing! Here are eight totally cringe-worthy ways for your player to shuffle off . . .

obody's perfect, are they? No matter how many hours of crafting you've put into Minecraft at the expense of sleep and sanity, it's all too easy for your character to die in ridiculously silly circumstances. If you've ever wasted a few minutes trolling a hostile mob in Creative mode, before accidentally switching to Survival and having it instantly kill you, you know what we're talking about. Then there's forgetting that you're down to a single heart of health and bumping your head as you ride a minecart; running out of armor and weapons durability while traversing the Nether . . . Minecraft sure is great at making you look stupid.

The eight outstandingly foolish deaths that we've listed have all happened to real players in actual gaming scenarios, and if you're anything like us, you might have experienced a few of them yourself! Never mind. If no one was watching, no one can prove it ever happened . . .

01

ANIMAL ATTACK!
Step this way . . .

Stand next to a cliff and admire the view. Ah yes — the sea, the sky, the lovely mountains . . . wait. What's this that has suddenly spawned next to you? Oh, it's a friendly, non-hostile pig or cow. How nice. Hang on, it suddenly pushed us off the cliff. Aaaaaagh! Yes, folks, this has actually happened in Minecraft to players unwary enough to stand too close to the edge of a cliff. An animal can magically appear out of thin air and knock you into the abyss. It's enough to turn any vegetarian into a bacon-munching meat freak.

02

PERILOUS PARKOUR
Might as well jump!

People attempting impossible leaps across car parks, rivers, canyons, and whatnot — and failing miserably — are everyone's favorite thing to watch on Youtube. It's no different in Minecraft, where we all think from time to time that we can jump like an Olympic pole-vaulter. So why do we keep on doing it? There's no way you can make that 200-meter leap from the top of that tower, to the roof of that woodland mansion . . . is there? Only one way to find out! Down you go, admiring the view in between multiple facepalms and cries of "But I thought I could make it!" before you go splat on the rocks below. Time to respawn!

03

TRADE OFF
Buy and die . . .

Newbies to Minecraft might well be aware that hostile mobs will react aggressively if you attack them, but most of them won't realize — until it's far too late — that even if you only try to trade with a hostile mob, it will probably fly into a rage and administer an instant beatdown on your player. We know, it's not fair. All you were trying to do was get that friendly-looking witch to sell you some dinner. How were you supposed to know that she'd go batpoop-crazy on you? Anyway, it's too late now: Next time you see a lady with a pointy hat, just keep on walking.

04

MODE NO YOU DON'T!

Switch it up

We've all been there. You're in Creative mode, zipping around your world with the greatest of ease. Is that a mountain in front of you? No problem, just fly over it. Is that an interesting-looking cloud formation over there? Why not float up and have a look? Feel like seeing the beautiful cityscape you spent all last week crafting from a mile up in the air? Well, why not? Just don't switch to Survival mode while you're up there. Ha ha, you'd never do that, would you? Oh . . . that's exactly what you did. Bye bye, then — see you at the bottom!

05

DIG IT!
Deep and distastrous

Come on, admit it. When you first started playing Minecraft and discovered that you could knock a block-sized hole out of the ground with a single click of a mouse, your first thought was "How deep can I go?" Smacking blocks out of the ground like a player possessed, you kept digging, deeper and deeper and deeper, until all you could see was the occasional soil-colored feature in the darkness. "Will I suddenly pop out into space . . . or, whoa, hell?" you thought excitedly — just before Minecraft automatically killed you for exceeding its permitted maximum depth. D'oh!

06
BOOM TIME
Take a step back

So you're delighted because you've just crafted the most evil trap in Minecraft history. The slime block, activated by the redstone trigger, will unleash a flood of lava on your buddy from behind the stone wall you've just built, as soon as they step on the detonator block. "What could possibly go wrong?" you ask yourself as you take a few steps forward to check out your handiwork. Just one thing, perhaps — you accidentally trigger your own trap, effectively committing Minecraft suicide. Ouch. That's got to hurt.

Press 'E' to inventory.

07

STEPPING OUT

Mind the gap

Build a house on the edge of a cliff, you say? Of course. What a fantastic idea . . . if you've read this far, you'll know what we're driving at, but for anyone who hasn't grasped what's about to happen, picture the scene. Your nice new house has been built near — or even better, directly facing — a cliff edge. Why not? The view is great. You open your front door after a good night's sleep, step outside to admire the view, and — whoops. Suddenly you're falling at terminal velocity toward the ground 400 yards below. You've just got time to wonder if your buddy removed the ground while you were asleep.

7:40 AM

Boss health

Read
Text 01

08

NETHER REGIONS
The booming bed!

Ah, the Nether. What an exhausting place to be, eh? All that fire and smoke, not to mention the hostiles roaming the sky, trying to shoot you. What you need is a nice nap. Build yourself a bed, lie down . . . and be suddenly annihilated as your bed explodes. Hardly a good night's sleep, is it? Yes, for some reason best known to the programmers at Mojang, beds are designed to blow themselves and their occupants to pieces down there in the Nether. Like the rest of the Minecraft universe, nothing in the Nether is as you'd expect — even your nightly resting place — so keep your eyes open, and try not to die while anyone's watching!

PROTECTING YOUR HOME

Made a killer home and want to keep away uninvited guests? Here's how to do it . . .

How many times has a Creeper blown up your house? Too many? What about other players coming and robbing your hard-earned loot? Fear no more, as we'll be showing you how to go about protecting your home by covering everything from the most obvious things, all the way to the most obscure ways possible.

One of the key factors when protecting a build is remembering to do the obvious and think outside the box. Mobs can be contained by sticking to what's already tried and tested, but when it comes to real human players, you need to get a bit crafty, simply because human players set on looting will likely know all the popular traps and therefore can avoid them with ease. But what they haven't planned on is you having this guide. To victory!

01

LIGHT IT UP

There is one surefire method to keep mobs away: Light. Even though during the day your only real threats are creepers and Endermen, when night falls, anything is fair game in the unforgiving world of OMG-Why-Are-There-So-Many-Mobs-In-My-World-Craft. To avoid getting overrun while you're working at night, lighting up the inside of your home or home area is the best way to keep mobs at bay. Torches are arguably the best light source in the game due to how easy they are to craft. Beacons have a higher light output, but when it comes to finding a beacon versus finding wood and coal, wood and coal win every time.

02

DIG A MOAT

Creepers are your biggest threat when it comes to keeping your home in one piece. But what happens to creepers when they're in water? Nothing. They explode, sure, but you won't take damage nor will any nearby blocks get blown to smithereens. If you don't fancy digging a moat all around your house, you could always mine up a three-wide trench leading to the house area with walls on either side so mobs are forced to cross into the water to get to you.

03

LANDMINES

This might be the easiest trap in all of Minecraft. Simply place a pressure plate on top of a block with TNT under it and that's your crude trap armed. Of course, don't arm landmines near your home area. Instead, place them sporadically around ten blocks away from your home in every direction. This will result in lots and lots of holes around where you live, but hey, at least there won't be as many mobs to bother you!

04

OBSIDIAN INSULATION

How do you get the better of an experienced Minecraft player? That's where obsidian insulation comes into play. For this, create rows of obsidian on the inside of your walls. Whenever another player mines through your wall, they'll need at least two blocks of height to be able to get in, right? So by adding the obsidian in this manner, it means that they will have to mine at least one block of obsidian if they want to get in. And as obsidian takes a whopping 13 seconds for you to mine with a Diamond Pickaxe, that will be plenty of time for you to line up some sweet headshots on the intruder.

05

FALLING TRAP DOOR

Picture this: You're walking along and see a chest. You open the chest, then the floor gives way and the next thing you know, you're eye-deep in lava! Create your very own falling floor trap to make sure that no creepers or mobs slip past your defenses and get close to you.

06

COBWEB DOORS

Slowing a hostile player down opens up a few options — you can hack them to pieces, or put a few arrows to their head. Create a doorway without a door in. We know, we know, it's weird, but it works. Then, instead of a regular door, drop in some cobwebs. When they attempt to go through the obvious entrance, they'll be slowed to a snail's pace, leaving them open to attack. Soul sand also works well for this one.

THE TRAPCRAFT MOD

Designed by Stewiecraft and ProPercivalalb, the Trapcraft mod adds in a selection of useful home protection devices, namely bear traps and training dummies. The bear traps can be used to stop mobs or animals in their tracks, while the training dummies act as decoys for most mobs — they will attack the dummies instead of going for the player. The pack also includes a fan to blow away items, a magnetic chest that pulls items to it, spikes for a pit trap, and a deadly fire-throwing machine. Pretty handy stuff, right? Right.

07

GOLEM DEFENSE FORCE

Iron Golems hit really, really hard, making them the strongest home defense unit out there. In case you don't know how to build them, here's a quick recap: Place four iron blocks in a T shape, then add a pumpkin as the head and presto change-o, an iron golem will spring to life. The only thing to keep in mind with these hardy brutes is they're not the smartest bunch. So if you've got a wall surrounding your homeland, be sure to spawn them inside it — spawn them outside and they have a habit of wandering off or getting themselves killed!

08 ANIMAL ARMY

Pets in Minecraft aren't just good for swimming in lava and shouting at when they sit on a block that's obviously going to end in their demise. Why, Mr. Fluffles? Why did you have to dive into lava when we repeatedly screamed at you to move? Ahem. Wolves are great for general mob defense, so that's killing skeletons and spiders, while ocelots are the perfect choice for chasing off creepers. No more random explosions!

09 DIG DOWN SLIGHTLY

Zombies can break through doors. Yes, it's all very annoying, but what they can't do is break down doors if they're not level with them. No, really, they're intelligent enough to break through doors with their fists but move them down half a block and they're utterly screwed. Keep this in mind next time you're building a house, and when you place the door, add in some half slabs below it and it's completely zombie-proof.

10

GIVING THEM WHAT THEY WANT

O kay, bear with us on this. Players attack because they want something, probably loot. So why not give it them, albeit with a dastardly twist? A moving floor trap works in a similar way to our falling floor trap. But instead of the floor falling into lava, the floor is pulled left and right by sticky pistons when a player mines up a specific block. In this case, use diamonds as the bait and when they mine it, they break a hidden circuit and go plummeting into, you guessed it, lava!

29

TRICKY TRAPS

Terrifying tricks to troll your friends

It's time to take revenge on all those mobs and griefers because this one's all about traps. We'll be covering a host of different types of traps, including simple three-minute builds, and builds that will take you a good few hours. Not every trap needs to be elaborate, you see, but sometimes going that extra mile and watching as that one skeleton that's been picking on you for days finally gets their comeuppance is hugely satisfying. We'll also take a look at everything from lava traps all the way to suffocation traps... which sounds a lot more morbid than it actually is!

01
MINECART DEATH TRAP

Lay down a minecart track, preferably leading into the distance so it appears like a regular minecart ride. Along the way, drop down a detector rail with a two-long trench. Fill the bottom of the trench with two layers of lava. Next, place a redstone torch to the right of the detector rail, with two sticky pistons facing the track one block back. Connect the redstone to the torch and cover the gap over and when someone takes a ride, they'll end up in lava!

02
MOVING FLOOR TRAP

Place two rows of flooring (we used stone bricks). Underneath the bricks, dig a deep hole directly below. Then one block away from both sides, place inward facing sticky pistons. Behind each of the pistons, add redstone repeaters. Trail redstone dust from each of the repeaters and curve it round behind. Place a block of your choice (maybe diamonds?) and pop a torch on the backside of it. When an uninvited guest comes along and mines the block, the floor will open and they'll fall in!

THE HOUSE TRAP

This build comes via Shiftyy, who came up with the idea of using a regular house to set the stage for an easy-to-build trap. The first thing you'll need to do is a build a nice, normal looking house. Then behind where the doors would go, dig a two-wide hole going over 20 blocks in depth. Head back up top and like our own moving floor trap, use sticky pistons on both sides of the hole so they extend and the floor appears like a normal floor. Drop some pressure plates in front of the door and you're all set.

03 DISPENSER TRAP

Put two iron doors next to each other, with a block to the right and two more above. Connect the redstone, with repeaters, around the side with the intention of building upward. Have one run of wiring going up and over, and another round to the side. Add dispensers filled with splash harming potion facing down above the two blocks, and pistons on both sides. The blocks cover the dispensers but because the pistons move the blocks, the potions will still connect, which allow the dispensers to remain hidden from view.

04 WATER TRAP 1

Mine up an area and in the dead center, create a two-by-two water-filled hole. With sticky pistons, create two L shapes on both sides. Behind the sticky pistons, lay down two, two-by-two platforms. Now pull out your redstone dust once more and run it along the bottom wall, around the right side, and halfway up the left and top sides. You should be left with a three-by-four empty L shape in the corner.

05
WATER TRAP 2

Now to make the redstone active. Drop down the repeaters as shown (and take note of their direction!). Then, in the corner with nothing in it, create a staircase leading up, around, and out. Add a redstone torch at the base of the staircase and connect it to the redstone. Lastly, run redstone up the staircase and on the final block, add in a button. Now build the door next to the button and test your water trap out.

06
DOOR TRAP

Not all traps need to be complex. Sometimes making the simplest of traps is enough to drive your foes into submission. For this trap, all that's needed is four iron doors and an iron pressure plate. Lay down the plate, then add four doors around it in a windmill fashion. When a player or mob steps onto the plate, the doors all close and they'll be stuck there with no immediate way out.

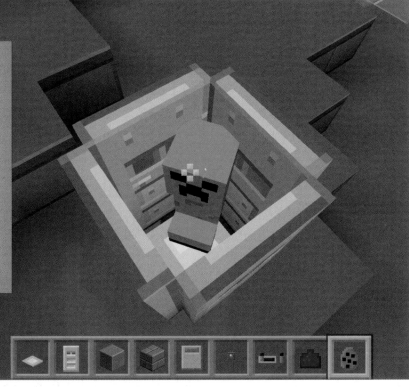

07 CHICKEN CATCHER TRAP

Raw chicken causes salmonella, which is why all chickens are evil. And because they're evil, it's totally ethical to catch them in traps in Minecraft. To build this, dig a T shape into the ground with redstone torches as shown. Drop a block in the middle, then a temporary block above. Add the wooden trap doors as shown, push three of the doors up, remove the temporary block, lay a wooden pressure plate, then just sit back and wait for your dinner to wander in.

08 EXPLODING TREE TRAP

Find an inconspicuous tree. Dig a four-by-four, four-deep hole underneath. Build a two-high spike in the center surrounded by redstone torches with a dot of redstone dust on the top of it. Put a lever on the underside of the tree and flick it once. Now dig four gaps in the pit's walls and fill with TNT. Cover over, and when someone starts hacking up the tree for wood, the whole thing will go KABOOM!

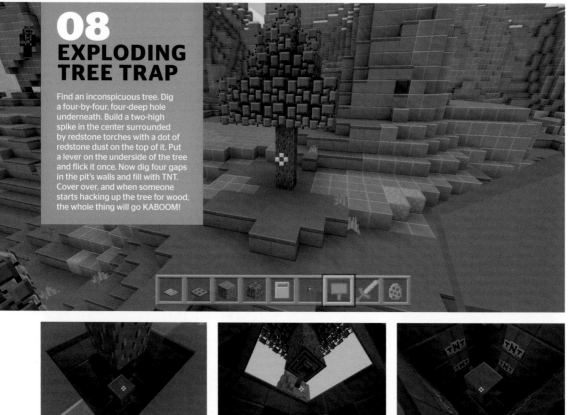

AMAZING MAZE

The ultimate security with little to no death

1 Kick things off by building the most generic house you can. You can, of course, build an extravagant house, but for simplicity, we'll be going with a fairly modest home. Ours is a mix of oak wood, oak planks, and oak half-slabs, along with stone bricks and stone brick half-slabs. Oh, and some dark oak fencing, oak steps, some torches, and two glass panes.

2 Next, arm yourself with a leaf block of your choosing. Now go on and run a square of leaves around the outside of the house one block out. From here, create a small entryway parallel with the front door and then start creating the shapes that will form the end section of the maze.

3 Start this next section by building up all the leaf blocks so they're four blocks in height or parallel with the roof of the house. Next you'll be matching the shape of the maze, just like we did in the last step, only on a larger scale. Once you've got all the twists and turns laid you're ready for Step 4.

4 Now to set the trap. At each of the dead ends, place a pressure plate in front of a dispenser. Next, pick a mob and fill each of the dispensers so when someone walks over the plates, they'll be met with a nasty surprise. To hide the dispensers, just use some carefully placed carpet.

5 With everything set up, all we need to do now is place a leaf roof over our maze area. It also might be worth adding some torches to the upper section of the house, just so from a distance, at night, the house illuminates the night sky and looks inviting. Little will they know all that awaits is feeling lost and mob battles. Mwahahahaha!

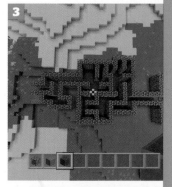

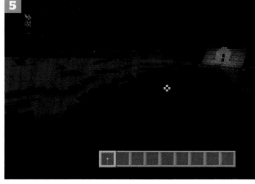

35

09
BURNING FEET TRAP

Place a trapped chest on the ground and mine one block below it, and dig up a three-wide, five-long trench. Add redstone dust under the chest and place a redstone torch on that block's face. Run a line of redstone from the torch to the end. Now add four upward-facing dispensers in each of the corners. Cover the floor and dispensers with black wool and black carpet, build up the walls, and when the chest is opened, lava will erupt around the player's feet.

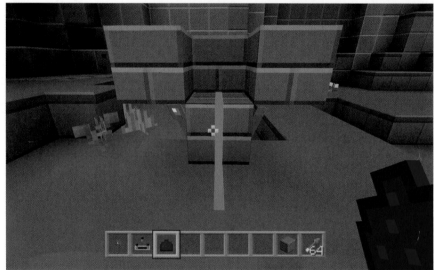

10
RAPID FIRE ARROW TRAP

Place down two rows of dispensers on top of each other and build a wall around them. Head to the back, and then add the lever block, repeaters coming from the dispensers, and the redstone dust as we have shown. A few blocks back, create the shape and add more redstone torches on the sides and back of the bottom block. Build an arm with a repeater on, connect the dust to the lever, and then you've got yourself a rapid-fire arrow minigun.

11
SUFFOCATION TRAP 1

Dig out a massive 18-long hole, five blocks deep into the ground. Three blocks from the bottom wall, in the center, run two rows of six blocks. Build the one-high walls, then the wall with a door frame on top at the Northern section. Create walls coming from the doorframe, then on the south side, another wall with flooring on top. Finally, drop down sticky pistons, then build two more rows directly above.

12
SUFFOCATION TRAP 2

In front of the two sticky piston walls, build two more walls from wood (these will be the floor). Next build two sets of arms on the sides of the pistons on both sides. Connect at the front, sloping underneath the door frame. Add in the redstone dust along the arms, a repeater on the backside, and then a torch on the right side. If in doubt, feel free to copy the accompanying image.

13
SUFFOCATION TRAP 3

For the final part, head back inside and lay an iron door with a button and give it a quick test. Behind the iron door, build a small room with something valuable in to lure people into pressing the button. Now all that's left to do is go back outside, cover over all the redstone with stone bricks, and create a nice temple look. The trick here is to make lots of steps and add a few pieces of fence and some torches.

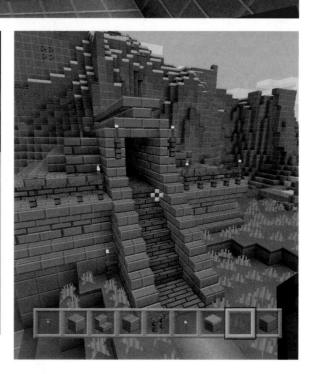

FIGHT & SURVIVE!

Our day-by-day Minecraft diary, written as we battled hostile mobs. Did we live to fight another day? Read on and find out . . .

Even a single day is a long time in Minecraft. There are monsters to fight, structures to build, and a whole lot of crafting to do, so if you do what we did and spend ten whole days battling for control of our own world in Survival mode, you'll know how much work we put in — and how much fun we had! Not that our adventure was easy. We made mistakes, we got things wrong and we didn't always know what we were doing — and for those reasons, we got killed by hostile mobs a lot. That's the beauty of the Minecraft universe, though: When your character respawns, it's your chance to learn from your previous mistakes and do things better this time. And after ten whole days of it, we like to think we'll do it faster, quicker, and more efficiently next time we click "Play."

DAY 1

When we arrived in our Minecraft environment today, it all looked pretty peaceful — but we've done this enough times to know that when you're in survival mode, anything can happen! Even the weakest enemy — like a spider or a creeper, for example — can jump out from behind a bush and suddenly you'll see that "You died!" red screen. So we built ourselves a secure place to live, complete with a bed to ensure a regular respawning point. Cool examples of buildings that are safe from home invasion are tucked into the side of a hill, or even have a moat, gate, and fences around them to keep pesky intruders out.

40

DAY 2

We woke up safe and sound in our new home on day two. Of course, no structure is going to keep villains out permanently — and anyway, we wanted to go out and explore the world — so the first thing we did was craft ourselves a cool weapon. We grabbed a wood plank and a stick from a disused house, mined an iron ingot and a cobblestone, and made a pretty effective-looking sword. A bow and arrow were next on our list. Who's going to mess with us now, we asked ourselves ... although as it turned out, our confidence was misplaced!

DAY 3

Today was a pretty tough day. While we were away from home, exploring a nearby woodland mansion, who should jump out from behind a door but a nasty old vindicator? These hostile mobs make a regular habit of attacking trespassers and can be pretty merciless, inflicting serious damage. Although we fought back with our trusty sword, we realized as the vindicator kept on smacking us around the head that we really should have spent some time crafting some armor. When we respawned back at home, getting some proper ironwear crafted was our first priority — helmet, chestplate, leggings, and boots.

41

DAY 4

As we approached the halfway point of our Minecraft vacation, we realized that we weren't going to achieve much unless we took weapons and combat tactics more seriously, so we invested solid time in acquiring materials for our crafting grid. We upgraded our sword from iron to diamond, which meant that we had to explore a lot of blacksmith chests and chest minecarts (which you can find in abandoned diamond mines) to get the necessary diamond. Once we were all set, we went out, found ourselves some big hairy monsters and taught them a lesson they won't forget in a hurry.

Your game mode has been updated▼▼▼▼▼▼▼

DAY 5

Today was all about combat. Spiders? Unpleasant creatures at the best of times, but when they're the size of a pony and hiss at you when they see you, they need a good talking to. Zombies? Not a problem. Creepers? Not that creepy — when you've got a diamond sword and armor like we have. As we secured the area around our HQ, ridding it of these irritating hostiles, we hummed a merry tune. That's what happens when you get proper protective gear on. In retrospect, maybe we were being a bit too confident — again! Can you guess what's coming next?

DAY 6

Today we were relaxing in the front garden when a horde of hostile mobs came out of nowhere and killed us. Now that's just not nice. We did our best, fighting off as many of them as we could, but even a diamond sword won't save you when there's a giant iron golem and a posse of zombies breaking down the garden fence. So we respawned and did some serious thinking. If we are going to make it through to Day 10 without getting killed all the time, we will need to master the noble arts of defensive home-crafting and making our weapons much stronger through enchantment.

DAY 7

Now that's what I call a busy day! Abandoning our nice (but vulnerable) home, we spent a few hours building what we humbly refer to as the ultimate fortress. We did an internet search for real-life megastructures and came up with a building that's a cross between a castle, a palace, and a big old barn. Check out these pictures for other cool examples. Once our epic new gaff was complete, we sat back and checked that no hostiles could get in. They tried, they failed — and how we chuckled. All we need now, we reckon, is to test out our new building and combat skills with a few other players . . .

DAY 8

Eight days into the Minecraft vacation of a lifetime, we opted for a multiplayer server. There's hundreds of them online. We chose one where we reckoned we'd have a good chance of crafting a diamond sword and gold armor. Once equipped with maximum butt-kicking gear, we swung into action, building a cool structure and battling anyone who tried to get into it. Minecraft is great on your own, but sometimes you need people to hang with, and a game shared is double the fun. Plus we learned loads about fighting enemies from other players. Collaboration is always good for you!

LG_Legacy

LG_Legacy

mgazda1 Wingman1106 mgazda1   Wingman1106

mgazda1   mgazda1

‹ Mies is afk.

DAY 9

Back in our saved world, we settled back into Ultimate Fortress HQ and considered how to finish our vacation in suitably epic style. We were still fighting off some pretty deadly hostile mobs, including a witch or two who flew into our territory and a crowd of evokers who tried to get us when we visited their woodland mansion. It was about time we created an ultimate warrior — an undefeatable ninja assassin who would have no problems with any of these mobs — and that's what we spent our day doing, with the help of mined and crafted materials. Day-glo costumes? We love 'em!

DAY 10

On the last day of our tour of duty, what better way to finish up than by battling the ultimate hostile mob — the Ender Dragon? Diamond sword in hand and enchanted armor on our back, we activated an End Portal in a stronghold, entered the End, and admired the view (it's pretty grim) before heading to the central island. Pausing to dispatch a few Endermen, we strode off to meet the dragon itself . . . who promptly killed us. After a few more attempts at fighting everyone's favorite reptile, we inflicted fatal damage on it and it dropped a dragon egg. That's breakfast sorted, then!

CONCLUSION
WHAT WE'VE LEARNED

Ten days in Survival mode would be enough to defeat the most experienced Minecrafter if they didn't take the necessary time to study building, crafting, combat, and mining skills. Make sure you find or build a secure respawning point so that you have time to learn how to do all these things without getting constantly beaten up by enemies. Invest in a killer set of armor and weapons, and make sure you have a large stock of crafting materials ready to go at all times. And remember — sometimes, you need to sit back and enjoy the beautiful landscapes. Isn't that the whole point?

FIGHT
TO SURVIVE!

A dozen killer PC mods which will make Survival mode tougher. Let's separate the miners from the minors!

Playing Minecraft on a PC? Then you're in for a treat. While we love mining on any platform, the ease of download and sheer range of mods available to laptop or desktop players lends our gaming a whole universe of new opportunities for innovation. Thanks to a huge online community, a massive number of mods can be searched out and investigated with no more than a couple of mouse clicks.

Of course, the internet is populated by malfunctioning, ineffective, or simply boring mods, so don't just download anything that takes your fancy. Read some peer reviews first, and expect some bugs every now and again. We like to refer to **www.minecraftforum.net**, for example, because new mods posted there come with screenshots and instructions. Check out this ultimate mods list for players who want their Survival games to be even tougher than usual!

01

ORESPAWN

Shock and ore!

Orespawn is one of the ultimate Minecraft mods if your objective is to engage in a battle to the death with a range of truly heinous monsters — and why else would you bother playing, eh? Sometimes you're just not in the mood for building a pleasant home in a forest; you want to take on a creature like Orespawn's frankly terrifying Doom Worm boss instead. Then there are dragons, krakens, dungeons, and something called Mobzilla that we're too scared to even look at, let alone fight . . .

02

CUBIC LUCKY BLOCK

Block rockin' beats

The makers of Cubic Lucky Block have included some truly amazing features in their mod, including a mighty range of hostiles for you to defeat . . . or be killed by! How about an entire army of ghost spiders, for starters? Or a platoon of runescape demons? And whatever Allosaurus and Nastysaurus had for breakfast, it's certainly turned them into tough opponents to beat. Never mind all that, though: the mod creators convinced us when they asked, "Have you ever want to see a Tower of Amethyst, Ruby, Uranium, and Titanium fall from the sky?"

03

GODZILLA

T-Rexstasy

The films, anime, novelisations, and now the Minecraft version of Japan's favorite rogue kaiju have all been based on one familiar vision: the massive foot of Godzilla stomping on a building and smashing it to smithereens. Translate that image to your favorite biome and you'll appreciate the fun that is to be had, as well as the sheer terror of trying to stay alive in this mod. Let's just put it like this — you won't be able to kill Godzilla with a bow and arrow.

04 MYTHICAL CREATURES

Creature feature

Swords that extend way beyond the reach of your normal blade? Armor that restores your health? Bows that shoot flaming arrows? Massive explosions that will take out any mob within several blocks? Take us there! That said, if your adversaries are the ones equipped with all this lethal kit, you might be the one on the receiving end rather than the player dishing it out. Well, you'd just better make sure you're ready for combat — and that's before we even get to the actual monsters of the mod's title . . .

05

TOUGH AS NAILS

Hammer time

Like an Ironman® triathlon equivalent for Minecraft, Tough As Nails earns its name through the increased difficulty that it offers the player, even in what might seem like a routine mission. Essentially, the people behind the mod have come up with ways to make a campaign in Minecraft trickier, thanks to innovations such as a thirst monitor (get to water at regular intervals, or you'll die) and a body temperature gauge (don't get too hot, or cold, if you want to live). Other cool features include regularly changing seasons, so make sure you pack a woolly hat.

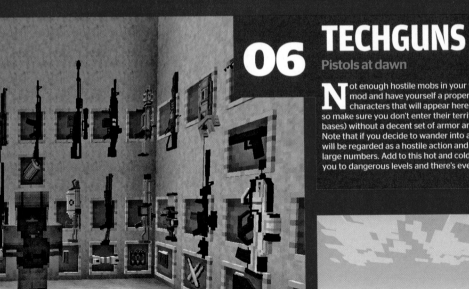

06

TECHGUNS

Pistols at dawn

Not enough hostile mobs in your world? Grab the Techguns mod and have yourself a proper war. The non-player characters that will appear here won't be slow to attack you, so make sure you don't enter their territory (in the form of military bases) without a decent set of armor and some serious firepower. Note that if you decide to wander into a base and steal the flag, this will be regarded as a hostile action and NPCs will swarm over you in large numbers. Add to this hot and cold biomes that will warm/chill you to dangerous levels and there's every reason to dive in.

COMBAT EVOLVED
Fight time

07

This tribute to first-person-shooter games such as Halo® is a fully immersive survival experience, requiring the player to contest various otherworldly NPCs of serious strength. Fortunately you're also equipped with super-cool weapons and armor, and you've also got access to a sweet vehicle or two which will get you around the map in style. New blocks include light emitters, and there are new ores to explore. Oh, and be careful with those nuclear weapons — they cause quite a bit of damage!

08 GEOMASTERY
Map it up

Like the real world, life in the Geomastery mod is nowhere near as easy and safe as it is in vanilla Minecraft campaigns. In real life, if you actually had to lift massive stone blocks and dig huge holes, you'd be there all week building a single wall. Now what Geomastery does that is so clever is make a crafting mission much tougher and slower than it would be elsewhere, so don't go in unless you're in for some hard work. Obviously the fun element is still there, though — it's not like you have to go down to homebase and buy a load of concrete or anything, right?

09 DEMONIZED
Speak of the devil

What the hey? Talk about a fight for survival. In the Demonized mod, you and your adversaries are equipped with a ton of terrifying firepower that would make an ordinary miner shudder. Take the Demonic Destroyer, for example — a lightning weapon that will roast people like Emperor Palpatine did, that time he gave Darth Vader the BBQ treatment. Then there's a sword called the Enchanted Scimitar, which burns targets as well as slicing them into pieces. The equivalent pickaxe is called the Bloody Breaker and outperforms its diamond counterpart, and then there's Blood Gem Armor, which has a ridiculous amount of strength. Add blood demons, Mutant blood demons and a four-armed monster called a squeamer and you're in for a hell of a mission!

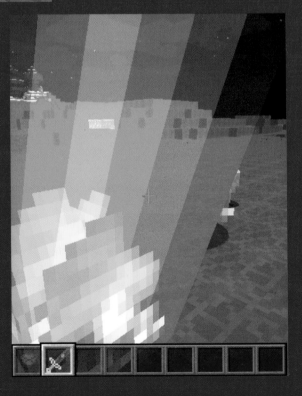

10 BETTER THAN WOLVES

Howling mad

Ready to play a really tough game? Try Better Than Wolves, which looks at first glance like a standard Minecraft game — until you try to sleep on a bed (there aren't any) or skip nighttime to get back to the safety of daylight (you can't). Those two factors alone make survival in BTW rather difficult. Add the fact that certain soft surfaces like grass or sand slow you down when you try to traverse them, plus a nightmarish spawn variation where your reborn character respawns a long way away from the original point, and you're in for a tough time of it. You're ready for that though, right? Good.

11

INVASION
Monster mash

Tired of building the ultimate fortress, ready to face attack by hordes of murderous hostiles, only to find that none of them ever arrive? Bored with preparing your structure for total warfare, only to find that the surrounding biome is devoid of enemies? Well, all that is about to change with the Invasion mod, where tons of evil mobs come out of the woodwork as time passes, forcing you to take them down or have your precious home leveled. We especially like the option to go away for a couple of days and then come back to face a massive crowd of baddies.

12

TRAGICMC 2
Tough talk

Now this is how to make Survival tough. Introduce 40 new hostile mobs and ten bosses, all of whom will happily stomp you to death as soon as they look at you. Introduce new blocks and weapons. Add 15 new potion effects, one of which is a health-sapper called cripple and another is called disorientation, which makes your field of vision tremble (aaagh!). Include a load of terrifying enchantments including vampirism (!) and the ability to shoot multiple arrows at the same time. Finally, add a new energy power-up called doom, which you can use to wipe enemies out in a variety of interesting ways. Ready for war? Let's have it!

STAY ALIVE
IN SURVIVAL MODE!

Want to become a master of Minecraft? Follow our tips and you'll go from novice to Survival expert in no time!

 reation might be a little scary at first, but there are few things as terrifying as trying to last the first night in Survival mode. As intimidating as it might be, this is way Minecraft is meant to be played, so learning how to survive is all part of the fun. Whether it's understanding the dangers of digging too far down (or digging up at all), learning when to eat certain foods, or creating an infinite source of water, there are loads of ways to keep ahead of the horrible creatures that come out when the sun goes down.

Whether you're a seasoned Minecraft pro or a first-time miner, we've got ten essential tips to help you dominate in Minecraft's Survival mode. So sit back, dust off your ender chest, craft yourself a trusty pickaxe, and prepare to master the art of block-based survival.

01

DIG THE RIGHT WAY

Without the safety net of Creative mode's god-like powers, there are new rules that need to be followed in order to avoid death in Survival mode. Here's a biggie that most new players forget — be careful when digging up or down. Digging straight down could lead anywhere, including straight down into a chasm or into lava. Digging down in a step-like pattern can help, but it will ultimately make you hungrier.

Digging upward can also be dangerous, mainly because blocks have properties in Survival mode that make them heavier. Since some blocks are heavy enough to crush you (or suffocate you), avoid it if you can to prevent nasty surprises.

02

TORCHES STOP SUFFOCATION

While it might be great for providing light in the darkest of places, the humble torch can actually save your life if you have to dig up. The item works a bit like a protective shell, since the game views it as a block.

So if you're digging underneath something like stone or sand, the falling bits and pieces won't suffocate you like normally. Torches can also be used to create temporary air bubbles when placed against a wall in the event of releasing water from above!

KNOW YOUR FOODS

03

One of the biggest things to consider in Survival mode is food and hunger. Surviving is a tough old business and you're going to need some chow in your belly to keep you going. However, different foods refill your hearts with different amounts, so eating something big to fill a single heart would be a total waste.

For instance, a steak will net you eight points, while a piece of raw salmon will refill only two. Don't eat your bigger or more nutritious snacks unless you're down to your last heart of health or so.

04 BEWARE OF GETTING TIRED

Staying alive in Survival mode means digging, smelting, building and more — all that hard work is going to require a lot of energy. However, working hard means you'll start to get a rumble in your belly. Since there usually isn't that much food in the first few hours of your adventure, working yourself hungry is far too easy.

To avoid wasting energy, try building roads or paths with slabs or stairs as this significantly reduces energy loss while walking or running. The stairs trick also works really well if you're trying to dig a stair mine, ensuring you don't waste away while digging deep.

05

INFINITE WATER SOURCE

One of the best ways to survive in the long term is growing your very own crops, and while you don't need water to make them grow, water makes them grow considerably faster. So dig a hole that's one block deep, one block wide, and three blocks long. Fill it with water and you can keep refilling your bucket from the middle block. Every time you do, the water on either side will refill the middle.

06

WATER BUCKET LIFESAVER

In Creative mode, you can fly and stop your fall with the tap of a button or the click of an analog stick. But in Survival mode, you won't have that luxury. In fact, you'll go splat if you fall from anything higher than 23 blocks!

Jumping into a body of water, such as a lake or ocean, will be enough to break your fall. However, since not every place you're exploring has such a thing, equip a bucket of water and throw it down beneath you as you fall for a safe landing.

07

ZOMBIE-PROOF YOUR DOOR

When night falls in Survival mode, the monsters come out to play. One of the most dangerous — and the most aggressive — is the zombie mob. They'll usually spawn near a house or village, and they'll immediately try to break in. Typical zombies!

To stop the undead from ruining your Minecraft party, try this little trick. Place your door on the side of the blocks that make up your door frame, rather than at the front of back. When it closes, the game will read the door as being open, and the zombie won't try to break it down!

08 COOK WITH FIRE

Food is really important when it comes to staying alive in the more dangerous version of Minecraft, and cooking your food will increase the number of hearts it will replace when you eat it. However, it can be hard to do this if you're in a hurry or just starting out.

Instead, why not try using fire to set animals such as pigs or cows aflame? As long as the animal is still burning when it dies, it will drop cooked meat instead of raw chunks, which is a great time-saver.

09 USE AN ENDER CHEST

Your inventory isn't the never-ending TARDIS it is in Creative mode, so you need to get clever when trying to survive. Since your inventory can only hold a limited number of resources, you'll probably want to make use of a special trick involving an Ender Chest.

Craft an Ender Chest, hit it with a pickaxe that's been treated with silk touch and you'll be able to fill it to your heart's content. Now you can destroy it and carry on with your game — when you craft another, all your items will be right there inside!

STOP LAVA WITH LADDERS

10

While it might not be obvious to new players, lava can be a really big problem if you're starting to mine deep for resources. It can also be a real issue if you're building a base underground to keep safe from mobs. That's where signs and ladders come in.

The game treats a ladder and a sign as a whole block, so if placed correctly, you can create what's known as a "lava trap." It's also a great way to provide lighting inside a cave or underground village. Just make sure there are no gaps in the trap!

TRAP ATTACK!

Defeat your enemies and ensure victory over the bad guys by setting these ten inescapable traps

P **icture the scene.** You're sitting in your shelter, enjoying a snack, and watching the pleasant landscape through your window. All is well with the world — until a hostile mob such as a zombie, creeper, spider, or skeleton (or much, much worse) decides to walk in.

At this point you have three choices: yell for help; start fighting; or sit back, relax, and laugh in mellow contentment as your adversary steps on the trapdoor you set up earlier in the middle of your floor, vanishes into the ground, and is never heard of again. We know which option sounds best to us. The noble art of setting traps is one that every self-respecting miner should learn. Why risk taking damage when you can dispatch your enemies — whether mobs or other players — with a little bit of forethought? Read on for ten killer trapping solutions!

01

THE BASICS

If you're going to catch the baddies before they catch you, you'll need to be well aware of the basics of trapping. This useful entry-level trap will get you rolling when it comes to nailing down those home invaders. You'll need a dungeon, decorated as evilly or cheerfully as you like, plus a mob spawner, which you can get/give or which can generate naturally. Fill the room with water by installing water source blocks, and escape the dungeon, filling in your exit route as you go. Check back for drowned mobs at intervals, and don't forget to pick up their drops!

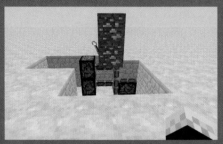

02

PISTON PACKIN'

Pistons — look into them! Any successful trapper knows just how easily these super-useful items can transform your snare from a good one into a great one. For example, a piston attached to a block can be designed to drop suddenly into a pit filled with a lethal substance such as lava — taking your target mob with it — when triggered by a switch activated nearby. A simple large holding pen might be the destination of the trapped mob if you want to keep it alive for farming purposes, too.

03

SANDY BUT HANDY

This ingenious trap uses the unique property of so-called slow sand — properly known as soul sand, and only found naturally in the Nether — to behave like quicksand and suck in any mob who walks on it. This trap model ensures two things: one, any mob that steps onto the sand can only progress towards the center of the trap, rather than out of it; and two, that escape is impossible because glass blocks of the right height have been placed at all exit points.

04

BAIT AND SWITCH

Sometimes the simplest traps are the best. Minecraft players are like everyone else, in that they're curious and always looking for ways to increase their resources. This trap takes advantage of every miner's tendency to turn a lever on sight, just to see what happens. The target player is motivated to use the lever even more by the promise of valuable booty in a chamber opened nearby. Associating entry to said chamber with the action of that tempting-looking lever, the victim takes the bait, activates the switch, and falls instantly into whichever dungeon you've got waiting for them right beneath their feet.

05 WATERY GRAVE

A powerful force in Minecraft is the hydraulic force of water. Release a jet of the cold blue stuff at a mob and, depending on its type, the liquid will push its target into trouble. One easy solution is to place a water trap at the top of a tower or near the edge of a cliff; ensure you've got access to the point where the mobs impact and drop resources. You can even guarantee results using a mob spawner — hey, a regular supply of goods every few minutes!

06 SKY'S THE LIMIT

Looking to maximize your mob-catching ability? Of course you are! Consider building your trap waaaaaaay high up in the sky, perhaps even as far up as the 255-block build height limit. This means that the maximum hostile mob count for your area (a sphere with a radius of 128 blocks from you) will be concentrated in your trap. You'll get many more mobs spawning at your trap, and falling prey to it, than you would at ground level, where subterranean caves might fill up with mobs.

07

HOUSE PARTY!

For ultimate peace of mind, build traps into every room in your house. Chests can trigger TNT when opened; blocks removed from walls, if players are motivated to do so with lying promises of treasure behind them, can release a sudden jet of lava; a water source block can be stashed immediately behind a door; or a special treat can be arranged for unwanted visitors under your bed. This could be a captive hostile mob such as a spider or zombie, a tamed wolf or two, or any evil beastie of your choice. Heck, why not stash a herd of spider jockeys right where you keep your diamonds?

08 CALL THE GUARD

So you've become a boss at this trapping lark by now? Congratulations — all you need to do now is refine your techniques so that nothing can escape your evil clutches. In this design, water flows downward so that any mob caught in the onrushing liquid is driven inexorably to a hole leading to a dungeon. On testing the design, it was found that mobs sometimes managed to jump out of the water in time to avoid their fate. The solution? Install a jump guard, an overhead ledge of rock that prevents jumping.

09 DOWN AND DROWNED

Note that even the best trappers sometimes need a backup plan if all else fails. After all, the hostile mobs in Minecraft weren't designed to go down without a fight, an expression which is literally true in the case of some water-based traps. Occasionally one will bob up and down in the water rather than have the decency to just drown, in which case an arrow to the head will come in useful. Glass blocks placed next to water also increase the downward flow for anything floundering around in it.

10 FALLING IN

Burning in lava or drowning in water are two very common ways to dispatch your enemies in the traps we've described, so why not combine the two? Of course, the two elements don't readily co-exist in vanilla Minecraft, but you can solve that issue by designing a waterfall which lands in a pool of lava. Your target mobs will spawn at the top of the falls, be carried along to the edge while taking possible damage along the way, take yet more health hits on the way down, and then be taken care of entirely by the lava. The catch? You'll need to build a massive structure to put all this in. Get mining, and happy trapping!

BUILD BONUS

RULE OF THREE

To achieve true greatness as a trapper, you'll need these three essentials. First, lava: Capture a source block which produces the stuff in the Nether, using a bucket. Watch your fingers! Then you'll need water, again most easily obtained with a water source block. Keep an eye out for the direction of its current, which is visible within it, and use it as a factor in your traps. Then there's everyone's favorite substance, redstone — found in chests, as drops from mobs, and generated by adding fuel to redstone ore. Apply this source of power to the moving parts of your traps for total invincibility!

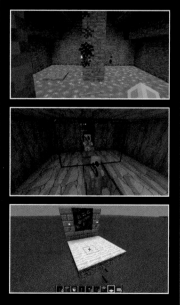

73

SURVIVORS' DIARY
MIDDLE AGES MASSACRE!

We fought a medieval-era battle and survived to tell the tale . . . barely. Here's how it all went down!

Modern technology is responsible for a lot of ranged weapons, isn't it? Guns, rifles, missiles . . . it almost makes today's methods of waging war seem a bit too easy. Look back 500 years to the medieval era, though, and you were a whole lot more likely to get skewered with a painfully sharp object, whether it was a sword, a spear, an arrow or a lance — so why would we bother putting ourselves through all that stuff in Minecraft? Because knights, warhorses, jousting, and hitting one another on the head with a mace is a lot of fun, that's why! Behold our day's worth of battle experiences in multiplayer mode, with our objective to storm and overtake a Middle Ages castle stuffed with soldiers, knights and even the occasional monster. Got your armor on, a set of arrows loaded in your quiver, and your rapier fully sharpened? Then let's go!

8 AM

SADDLE UP

Before we do any fighting, of course, we're going to need a trusty steed and some weapons to play with. For this medieval bash we've made sure that a sword, bow, and arrow, and full set of armor are forged and ready for war, while our warhorse is tamed, fed, rested, and up for a bit of serious fighting. Let's get to the barracks as soon as possible, where we'll be meeting the rest of our soldier buddies. Getting those lazy swines out of bed and onto the server this early in the day has been a struggle, believe us, but it'll be worth it when the swords start swinging. Portal blew up. Typical.

9 AM

REGIMENT — ATTENTION!

Time for parade — so let's get the team together. Today we've got soldiers of all types, wearing whatever uniforms they want. Sure, we hardly look like a real army, but who needs rules, eh? As long as we pull together, stand against the enemy on this server, and help one another out of a critical spot, victory will be ours! Well, that's what we tell ourselves as we organize into fighting groups — it's the only way to get past the pre-battle nerves that are starting to make themselves felt. Can we really defeat a rival army, take a castle, and overcome a king and his knights? Only one way to find out . . .

9:30 AM
TIME TO CHARGE!

That's enough standing around and chatting; it's time to fight. We draw together in a battle group, dividing up tasks among us. We're planning to power through the foot soldiers in the opposing army, taking down players in one-to-one combat and forcing the enemy to withdraw into the safety of the castle. After they've got the drawbridge up, we besiege them and figure out a way inside. Once in the fortress, we'll work our way to the throne room and capture the flag. Sounds like a plan — and now we can see our adversaries massing in the distance. Ready? Set? Chaaaaarge!

10 AM

ONE ON ONE

Aaagh! Someone's chopped our arm off ... But as the Black Knight in *Monty Python* said, it's a mere scratch! We're deep in a melee now, working our way through individual combats and taking damage. Ouch! That soldier just bashed us on the head! But we've recovered and dealt him fatal damage with our sword, which — fortunately — we remembered to forge from diamonds in our last campaign. Now we're moving onto a huge mob, a player sporting a serious set of armor. Can we defeat them without dying? Hmm ... Better try a bow and arrow for this one; it's much safer.

12 PM

BESIEGE ENEMY CASTLE

Well, that was exhausting. Battling several dozen players with close-range weapons has left our right-clicking finger completely numb. Just as well they've got the message and retreated into their castle, raising the drawbridge, lowering the portcullis, and leaving us to set up camp outside. It's a waiting game now. Every now and then, one of their soldiers comes out and challenges us to single combat, and we scare them off. We need a plan to get inside the castle, though, or we'll be here all day. It's no use trying to climb the walls. What about going in under them?

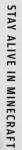

1:30 PM
INVADE THE DUNGEONS!

After a bit of digging at the lower edge of the castle walls, we're in! The dungeons stretch ahead of us, with no obvious way up and out into the open area behind the walls, so we're going to have to tread carefully. Our enemy are a cunning bunch and no doubt they've built traps for us, and we'll also have to watch out for sudden lava outbreaks this deep in the ground. Our troops lead the way through the darkened chambers, looking for an exit. Although we fight off the occasional zombie and spider, all is silence and gloom . . .

5 PM

FACE THE CHAMPION

Jousting completed, we return to face the enemy king; although we've taken some damage at the hands of his favorite horseman, it's nothing that a quick snack won't fix. But before we get to take His Majesty on in single combat, he laughs evilly and gestures toward a hidden doorway. In a trice, the biggest knight we've ever seen leaps out toward us, waving a massive diamond sword and uttering a war cry. Behold the royal champion, a fighter who thinks nothing of killing an entire platoon of soldiers before breakfast. Perhaps we should run away? Too late! He's attacking us . . .

5:30 PM

BATTLE DRAGONS!

Well, that was pretty tiring. Killing that giant knight took every bit of skill we had — and just as we turn from his defeated figure to the king, what happens? Why, the devious old monarch spawns a pair of monstrous dragons! Surely that's not fair, we start to say, as the two warlike lizards begin to eat our players. Fair or not, there's only one thing for it, and we jump into battle like players possessed. Swords, arrows, pickaxes — whatever we have to hand, we use, and slowly we gain the upper hand against the monsters, although they singe us a bit before we defeat them . . .

7 PM

KILL THE KING

Soldiers, knights, champion, and now pet dragons dead or dying, the king of our enemies now has nowhere to go — and cowering against the wall, he begs for mercy. After smacking him around a bit just for good measure, we agree to let him live in return for his unconditional surrender. After all, there's no harm in showing a bit of generosity in victory . . . We grab the enemy flag from the topmost turret of the castle and plant our own instead, signifying that whoever you are, we'll never be defeated! And now for a nice cup of tea . . .

CONCLUSION

THE BATTLE ROYALE!

So what have we learned from our epic day of warfare? One, never underestimate your enemies. The team we were fighting against today really knew their stuff — building traps, holding out against a siege, preparing obstacles such as jousting tournaments, training up a huge champion, and even spawning dragons. Two, take as many weapons with you as you can carry; you never know which ones you'll need in a critical situation, and it's impossible to predict which hostile mobs are going to leap out of the woodwork. Finally — never give up. A seemingly impossible scenario in Minecraft will always be resolved with enough patience — and courage!

MINI BUILDS

Build amazing things in minutes!

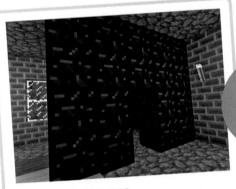

BUILD A PANIC ROOM

1 SET THE WALLS
Pick your location and construct your panic room's walls from a blast-resistant block such as obsidian. Don't forget to replace any external walls or ceilings if needed! Leave a small doorway.

2 MOTION SENSOR
Replace one floor-level block from your walls with a redstone lamp, and add pressure plates around the outside of your room. The lamp will act as an alarm, warning you if anyone is standing outside.

3 LAY THE REDSTONE CIRCUIT
Start off facing the redstone lamp head-on, and lay a trail of redstone along the floor back to each pressure plate. It's important to start at a 90-degree angle to the lamp to connect the power.

4 FILL IT UP
Once you've tested that your pressure plates light up the lamp, add some chests to your panic room and fill them with food, supplies, weapons, and enough obsidian to block up the doorway behind you. Feel safe yet?

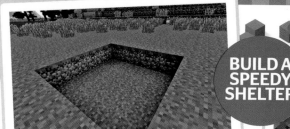

BUILD A SPEEDY SHELTER

1 DIG A SMALL PIT
Going underground means you don't need to make walls, so we're heading downward for this shelter. To start off with, find a clear area and dig a 4x4 block crater one block deep.

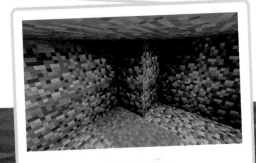

2 PIT-CEPTION
Excavate down two blocks farther in the center of your crater. This is as deep as you'll need to go, and the shallower edges will mean you can get a roof over your head as quickly as possible.

3 GET IN THE HOLE
Hop down into the deepest part of your shelter and add a roof above your head, working inward from the corners. We've used stone here, but almost any block will do in a pinch.

4 LET THERE BE LIGHT
Place a torch or two in the corner to brighten things up, and then dig one block outward from each of the walls. You'll now have the four-by-four floorplan you laid out — just enough space for a one-night hideaway, should you ever need one.

5 SPEND THE NIGHT
Once you're holed up for the night, you might as well make the most of it. Place a crafting table and a bed — you can get in a few chores before hunkering down for a snooze until morning.

FIGHTING OFF THE HOSTILES

Hostile mobs are pesky, dangerous, and always in the way. Here are ten of the most irritating!

Just when you were enjoying a sunny day in Minecraft and planning to build a castle made out of glass and diamond to impress your significant other, here they come — a pack of enemies, or hostile mobs as we call them. What's a Minecrafter to do? Well, show them who's boss, for starters! Hostiles in the Minecraft universe range from the fairly inoffensive — spiders, zombies and so on —

to the heinously aggressive. We've compiled a list of ten of these annoying beasties for you, together with scores based on how likely they are to kill you and whether the materials that they drop when you defeat them are any good. In each case you'll need a very reliable sword and armor at the very least; if you're wise, you'll invest some time and resources in crafting protective gear and weapons of gold or diamond quality. Let the battle begin!

44 36 64 62

01

CREEPER
Green and gaseous

One of the most common enemies you'll encounter in the Minecraft universe is the creeper, a tall green mob with a nasty habit of suddenly appearing from behind trees and whatnot. Their exact colors may vary slightly, but basically they look like an armless biped with a sad expression. Annoyingly, they'll explode within three blocks of you, hissing as they approach: Fortunately you'll get a few seconds to attack one before it explodes. If you're really lucky, a creeper will drop a music disc — or its own head — when you kill it. Which you should.

DAMAGE INFLICTED? Varies
DROP QUALITY 3/5

02

ZOMBIE
The undead rise

The designers at Mojang must be keen fans of *The Walking Dead*, because there are loads of different zombie variants in Minecraft. From a common-or-garden undead chap, to a zombie villager, to a baby zombie villager, to a chicken-riding armored baby zombie villager (we kid you not), there are enough reanimated dudes stumbling around the place to infect an entire planet. It's your job to stop that happening. Fortunately, they don't inflict much damage, so get your sword out and return them to their original condition, i.e. dead.

DAMAGE INFLICTED? 2/4
DROP QUALITY 2/5

03

GHAST
Ghastly times ahead

These massive flying cubes would be quite nice to look at, as they billow through the sky overhead, if they didn't shower you with fireballs. They can see you even if you're 100 blocks away. Have your bow and arrow ready to take them out at long distance, or lure one into a low-ceilinged room where you can stab it. Look out for a Ghast Tear, which can brew potions.

DAMAGE INFLICTED? 9/25
DROP QUALITY 3/5

04

VINDICATOR
Warning: dangerous mansions

Woodland Mansion-dwellers the vindicators are an unpleasant lot, dying to batter you with an unpleasant-looking axe. The axe in question may well be enchanted, in which case you're really in trouble. The obvious way to avoid them would simply not to enter any mansions, attractive as these structures definitely are. That said, vindicators often drop emeralds and axes when you dispatch them, so don't be afraid to take them on.

DAMAGE INFLICTED? 7/19
DROP QUALITY 3/5

05

EVOKER
Fangs a lot

As well as the vindicators, woodland mansions are also the home of evokers. They'll attack you using evoker fangs — nippy traps that suddenly rise up out of the floor and bite you, believe it or not. The fangs either appear in a straight line, radiating from the evoker to you, or in a ring around the evoker. Not only that, the evoker can summon a mini-enemy called a vex, which flies around the room like an annoying mosquito while shooting at you.

DAMAGE INFLICTED? 6
DROP QUALITY 3/5

06

WITCH
Room with a broom

A witch is an unusual mob, defending itself by throwing potions of weakness, slowness, and harm at you and also healing itself with magic brews. You definitely want to attack one if you see it, though, because the great thing about them is that they drop a large number of useful items. These include spiders' eyes, which are handy for brewing potions of your own.

DAMAGE INFLICTED? Varies
DROP QUALITY 5/5

07

GUARDIAN
Waterborne and worrisome

The repulsive-looking guardian may spawn and live underwater, specifically near ocean monuments, but that doesn't stop it leaping onto the shore and squeaking angrily while trying to attack you. Defeat one and you'll be rewarded with one or more of several possible drops, including prismarine shards or crystals, raw or cooked edible fish, and inedible seafood such as puffer fish. Watch out for those spikes now, and that single evil eye!

DAMAGE INFLICTED? 2/9
DROP QUALITY 4/5

08

WITHER SKELETON
Making no bones . . .

Sure, the Wither Skeleton looks like a spooky, blackened version of a normal skeleton — but it's far more dangerous. Annoy one and it'll shoot you with the wither effect, a health-depleting spell that causes you to lose a heart every two seconds. And it has a nasty great stone sword, too, so approach these hostiles with extreme caution. On the other hand, they tend to drop useful stuff when defeated.

DAMAGE INFLICTED? 4/10
DROP QUALITY 3/5

09

SLIME
A slippery customer

This green cube will hop toward you and fight in melee fashion in the absence of weapons, and its slime can still kill you. Don't run away from a slimy fight: On defeat, they may drop a slimeball, which is an integral ingredient in slime blocks and pistons. These are massively useful in building structures and traps, so when you see a slime mob, don't hesitate to engage with it.

DAMAGE INFLICTED? 2/4
DROP QUALITY 1/5

10

SPIDER JOCKEY
Double yuck

Dropping items such as string, bones, and arrows on death, this repellent combo of oversized galloping arachnid and reanimated calcium will put up a serious fight before you get to pick up the goods. Because the spider and its rider (Hey! that rhymes) will both attack you simultaneously, you'll need to be well armored and equipped with weapons to take one on. Achieve this feat, though, and you'll be among the very best of the very best!

DAMAGE INFLICTED? 6/13
DROP QUALITY 5/5

AH, AH, AH, AH,
STAYING ALIVE!

We count down the best ways to steer clear of Minecraft's main hazards

What are the best things about Minecraft? The awesome things you can build, creating your own world, exploring the amazing creations of other people? If the best bits about Minecraft are to do with creating, then definitely the worst are to do with destroying — mostly monsters destroying everything you've worked hard to build up, or even your own health meter! It can be so annoying if you've spent ages creating an incredible castle or traveling to explore the areas in the Discovery Update, all to have it spoiled by a mean monster. Luckily these monsters have their weaknesses like anybody else and can be taken down and fended off. So if you want to keep creepers and endermen at bay, here are the smartest tips for staying alive while enjoying the wonderful world of Minecraft.

WEAR YOUR ARMOR

01

The first thing you need to make sure you protect is yourself. Creepers are notorious for sneaking up on you and exploding when you least expect it. You can craft armor from leather, gold, iron, or diamond and make helmets, chestplates, leggings, or boots. Armor can also be dropped by skeletons and zombies, so if you kill one, remember to pick its armor up! Or, if you're really lazy, just buy some! If you're attacked, the armor will take the damage, rather than you, until it loses durability. Then it's up to you to fight or flee!

02 BE ENCHANTING

No, we're not saying sweet-talk the monsters into not destroying you. Enchanting your armor gives it certain powers that can help in a variety of dangerous situations. Blast protection, for example, reduces damage from explosions, while protection will make each hit on you slightly less effective if something is attacking you. Go to an enchantment table or an anvil and use your armor with an enchanted book for an extra layer of safety against the rampaging hordes.

Diamond Chestplate (#0311)
Thorns II
Unbreaking II
Protection III

Enchanted Book (#0403)
Thorns II

Repair & Name
Diamond Chestplate

Enchantment Cost

Diamond Chestplate (#031
Thorns III
Unbreaking II
Protection III

03 GET TO WATER

If you're scared of being attacked by an Enderman, make sure you are close to water. These hostile mobs are damaged by water, so if one is attempting to attack you and teleporting all around, jump in a boat. That way, when the enderman is teleporting around you, it will keep getting damaged by the water, helping you defeat it easily and ensuring you take less damage. If you can use your bow on them to keep distance between the two of you, that's even better.

04 BUILD A ROOF

Your character is two blocks high. An enderman is three blocks high. This may seem like they have an advantage, but you can use it to yours. If you're out in an area you're likely to be in for a long time, build a roof that is three blocks up. That way you can move around easily, but if an Enderman rushes you, it'll knock its head on your roof block. It won't be able to get into your lair, meaning you can shoot it with your bow and arrow at your leisure.

05

HEAD UPWARD . . .

If you're building a home, build it high! That way at night you can keep a good eye out for any hostile mobs that may be on their way to ruin your fun. It'll also take the monster longer to reach you, giving you more time to ready your weapon and stay safe. There are only a few creatures that can climb ladders as well, so it'll reduce the number of things that want to kill you being able to reach you.

06 ....OR HEAD DOWNWARD

Night is the worst time for all those mobs to spawn and search out sleeping players to attack, so heading underground and mining throughout the night could be your smartest bet. Monsters don't like fire, so if you're underground, light plenty of torches to guide your way and keep those creepers and zombies away from you during their most active time. This will keep you safe and maximize your output while everyone else is sleeping and being attacked!

07 DISGUISE YOURSELF

Now, the Enderman is a generally passive mob, just staring creepily at you until you go away, but it can get aggressive if you get too close and is super annoying when it moves the blocks you've carefully placed for a construction. So they have to die. One trick for keeping the enderman passive is to wear a pumpkin helmet. It won't attack you if you place the cursor over its eyes, nor will it teleport away when attacking it. This takes away the enderman's main fighting advantage, helping you to stay safe or kill it more easily.

SECURE YOUR HOME

08

Another way to stay safe at night is to make your home an impenetrable fortress, which doesn't actually require that much special work. Hostile mobs aren't able to spawn in a room that is entirely built with walls that have been created from player-made blocks. So as long as you have constructed it entirely yourself and left no gaps, mobs shouldn't be able to spawn and get inside your property, making a self-built home as safe as houses.

ATTACK THE LEGS

09

If you are brought into combat with an enderman and have no water nearby or pumpkin heads to put on (and to be honest, it's your own fault you've been so careless as to go out without your pumpkin head), then either attack from distance with your bow and arrow or go for the legs. Attacking an Enderman's legs stops it from teleporting, making it a straight one-on-one battle, rather than a one-on-one-in-multiple-locations battle, improving your chances of survival.

GET A GOLEM 10

Whether you find a spawned one or have to make one yourself by stacking three iron blocks in a row, a fourth underneath the middle one and topping it with a pumpkin head, iron golems are massively useful attack dogs. Any hostile mob that comes within 16 blocks will incur the wrath of the iron golem and will get attacked with ferocious power. These are incredibly handy to have around as they can be on the lookout for hostiles while you get on with your daily tasks. And who doesn't love to see a creeper getting crushed?!

PLAY IT SAFE

Minecraft does offer some cool and creative combat alternatives

There are a few options if you don't want to build something or do battle. Run! Double-tapping the forward button gives you a burst of sprint speed so you can run away from pretty much all attacking hostile mobs. If you want to play it even safer, use Peaceful Mode, which completely gets rid of hostile mobs and lets you play your game in peace and quiet without fear of being attacked by skeletons or having your property damaged by creepers and Endermen. But, let's be honest, who wants to live in a virtual world without just a little bit of danger?

BEWARE! MEGA BITES

If you go down to the map today, be sure of a big surprise . . . dangerous animals!

If we've learned one thing from the hundreds of hours we've put in while roving around the Minecraft universe, it's that it doesn't owe us an easy ride.

No character, whether player or mob, is there to make life easy for us — and while we all know that hostile mobs are all over the place, just dying to make our Minecraft experience miserable, few of us ever take the time to think about the natural (or unnatural!) fauna that we're likely to meet along the way.

Now, the vanilla Minecraft game certainly comes with its share of two-legged, four-legged, and eight-legged nasties (get off me, evil spider!) but you can make things even more challenging, zoologically speaking, if you install one of many mods specializing in animal characters. If you do this, make sure you've got plenty of weapons to hand — and if not, let's just say you'd better be a fast runner.

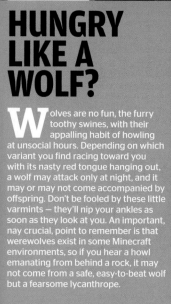

01

HUNGRY LIKE A WOLF?

Wolves are no fun, the furry toothy swines, with their appalling habit of howling at unsocial hours. Depending on which variant you find racing toward you with its nasty red tongue hanging out, a wolf may attack only at night, and it may or may not come accompanied by offspring. Don't be fooled by these little varmints — they'll nip your ankles as soon as they look at you. An important, nay crucial, point to remember is that werewolves exist in some Minecraft environments, so if you hear a howl emanating from behind a rock, it may not come from a safe, easy-to-beat wolf but a fearsome lycanthrope.

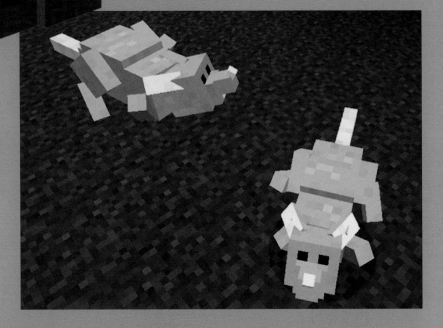

02

FEELING A BIT RATTY

What's that scuttling around near your feet, tickling you with its whiskers? You'd better hope it's a mouse, completely harmless in Minecraft and also rather cute. If you're unlucky, though, it'll be a rat that is scampering across your sandals. These frankly unhygienic rodents will not only try to bite you, but their mates will come running, too — and before you know it you'll be surrounded by a pack of them. Kill them, grab the coal they drop, and run.

BEARING UP

03

Who doesn't love a nice, cuddly bear? Anyone who has been stalked by a massive, slavering polar bear through a snow biome in Minecraft, that's who. Note that brown bears are much nicer to be around; they only attack you if you attack them first, which seems reasonable to us, and they drop fish, which is handy. Their arctic cousins are much less chummy, though, so if you see what looks like a giant snow block running at you, prepare for battle.

TOOTH TIME

04

Just when you thought it was safe to go in the water … Well, actually, it's never safe to go in the water in Minecraft — unless you're in Creative mode, of course. In any other mode, if you decide to go for a swim and you come up against a shark, you're in trouble. These toothsome beasties will attack anything they encounter, player or mob, although there are two clear benefits to taking them on. First they drop shark eggs, which you can use to spawn baby sharks, which you can then tame to attack everything except you. Second, you can use shark teeth to craft chainmail. Handy, eh?

05
RAYS OF LIGHT

Stingrays, deceitful creatures that they are, have a nasty habit of hiding in sand near the edge of the water while you're on land. Step into the water, though, and they'll attack you in about three seconds, trying their best to poison you. Don't confuse them at any costs with manta rays, which are great animals that float around the place looking elegant, and that will never (as far as we know) try to poke you with a painfully sharp tail.

06
GLOWIN' DOWN

Jellyfish are totally untrustworthy. They're so untrustworthy, in fact, that it's time for us to invoke a metaphor. Remember that super-good-looking guy or girl at school who looked great but was actually really mean? That's a Minecraft jellyfish to a T. These blobby creatures are luminescent at night and look truly incredible — get some in your swimming pool if you can. Get too close to one, though, and it'll jab you full of poison. What's more, they look worryingly like ghasts.

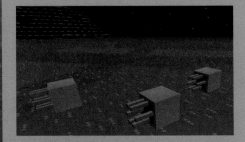

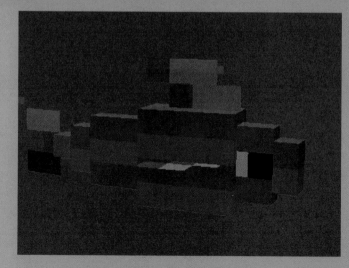

07

FISHY GOINGS-ON

Just like the real world, piranhas come in several types — in Minecraft, there are 11 of them to look out for. Small, unassuming, and generally nothing to worry about until they start biting giant chunks off you, these fish will lurk under the surface of a given lake or ocean, lazily keeping track of you — until you submerge. At this point, they will suddenly accelerate to a hideously great speed, lunge at you, and turn you into lunch. Best stay on the beach this time.

08 THE CLAW STRAW

Scorpions, repulsive stingy creatures that they are, come in several types in Minecraft, depending on which mod or server you're on. We've come across green-and-brown ones that do the familiar trick of poisoning you to death with that nasty, stabby tail of theirs. Then there's a blue type that you encounter in winter biomes, which freeze you. Finally the Nether has its own set of scorpions — red ones, of course — that set you on fire. Note that when you kill them, they drop up to three babies, which are too small to defeat easily. Not to be confused with easily beatable spiders at any cost.

09 PIGGING OUT

We all love Minecraft's nice, pink pigs, don't we? Well, here's a rather less lovable version — the wild boar, recognizable by its brown coat and set of white fangs hanging out of its almost entirely unappealing face. Unlike the aforementioned pink piggies, a boar will fight back if you attack it, and is highly likely to do you some serious damage. On the other hand, you'll be rewarded with pork chops if you defeat one, so sharpen your sword and keep your BBQ ready!

10

ON A ROLL

Crocodiles, in Minecraft as in real life, are essentially long, green death-tubes with far too many teeth at one end, and a tail at the other that is capable of knocking your head off. They're extremely fast on land or in water, tend not to die easily, and have a terrifying attack technique — the death roll — that is a nightmare to escape. If it grabs you and starts spinning, you'll find it hard to inflict damage, so why not save time and just run away if you see one? Then again, the braver miners among you will enjoy the green leather they drop when you kill them — perfect for crafting armor.

BONUS BOXOUT

MORE BEASTIES, BOYS!

Many of the unfriendly animals that we've described on these pages can be found in the Mo'Creatures mod (**www.mocreatures.org**), a fun Minecraft environment where no map is complete without a swarm of organisms to defeat. Along with the animals described here that you'll also find in real life, the Mo'Creatures mod also includes ogres of various levels of lethality, and the usual hostile mobs. Make sure you're well equipped with armor and weapons before you embark on a campaign in this highly dangerous universe — after all, pretty much everything you'll meet there is out to get you!

THIS IS
THE END
MY FRIEND...

If you want to complete your Minecraft mission, you'll need to survive the End. Here's how!

Minecraft veterans will always argue about the relative merits of Minecraft's three dimensions. The Overworld is all very well, they'll complain, but where's the danger? Where's the challenge? Okay then, their buddies will say — how about the Nether? There's plenty of hostile mobs and other perils down there. Yes, comes the answer, but it's easy to get through the Nether without so much as a singed big toe!

What players always agree on is that the third Minecraft dimension — the End — is not to be trifled with, at least if you're outside Creative mode. Head down there, as you'll have to sooner or later if you want to complete a standard Minecraft campaign, and you'll be faced with a bevy of monsters that would make anyone quiver in terror. But have no fear, readers — we're here to help! Read on for our definitive guide to how to survive Minecraft's spookiest dimension — and even do rather well down there . . .

01
WE'RE GOING UNDERGROUND!

They're wings that let you glide through the air, which is great for avoiding fall damage from high places. It's also just a fun way to get from A to B, and having them up on your back really opens up new ways to explore the world.

Unlike actual wings, you can't use them to gain height on their own, but if you combine them with fireworks to propel yourself forward then you can zoom across the sky like a superhero. More on that later.

You place them in your chest armor slot, so you won't be able to equip them at the same time as your favorite diamond chest piece, unfortunately. They're difficult to obtain, but don't worry, we'll walk you through that next.

02
TAKE IT ALL IN

Once you've arrived in the End, it's worth taking a moment to accustom yourself to your new surroundings. Things in the End don't behave like they do elsewhere; for example, there are fewer mobs around; most of the block types you're used to don't exist down here; the landscape is dominated by purpur and end stone blocks, hence the purple and sand color theme; and there's a very real chance that you'll be killed any second by a fiend from above (more of that shortly). Equip your best weapon — you're going to need it — and consider constructing an emergency safety chamber underground while you figure out what to do next. Don't worry, though; you're in safe hands with us. We're going to have some serious fun down here.

03

ENDEAVOUR TO END ENDERMEN!

You'll have seen the odd little dark figure wandering about in the distance — well, you'd better hope that they stay over there, and that a whole posse of them don't decide to come over and pay you a little visit! These are the dreaded Endermen, spooky creatures with malevolent gazes that can't wait to cause problems for you. They usually spawn in packs of four, and while they're neutral by default, you literally only have to look in their direction and they'll perceive that as an attack — in which case, it's game on. They will teleport both toward and away from you, shuddering with rage, and can also step up a block's height into the air without needing to jump. Defeat them, though, and they drop the much-coveted ender pearls.

04

ISLAND HOPPING

You'll have noticed in your first few minutes in the End that the dimension is composed of a large central island and loads of smaller Outer Islands, over there in the distance. Do you want to have a look at them? Of course you do! Unfortunately you can't swim over there, but there's a ready-made solution available. Chuck an ender pearl into one of the Gateway Portals you see around the place, and you'll be teleported the 1,000-block distance to the Outer Islands, where you can get up to all kinds of interesting mischief. These islands generate infinitely, complete with all sorts of cool features, so you're unlikely to run out of things to do over there. You almost wonder whether it's worth coming back!

05 GET YOUR WINGS

When it was announced a while back that Mojang was introducing a flight option called elytra to Minecraft, players lined up to investigate. After all, what could be better than soaring above the waves or terrain with the greatest of ease? Grab a pair of elytra from the end ship and strap them on (see below); in essence, these leathery wings enable the player to glide rather than fly, but with the aid of a firework (or a flying mod) you'll be jetting along with the best of them. Note that you won't take damage while flying unless you smack right into a mountain or other large object, so keep your eyes open; your hitbox is also half the usual height while flying. Don't get cocky, though; it's a long way to fall!

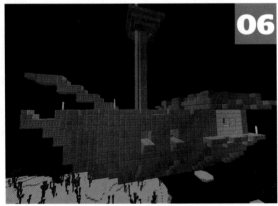

SHIP AHOY, CITY SLICKERS!

Although the End seems eerily uninhabited at first sight, swarms of endermen aside, it seems that life was once rather busy in this spooky dimension. Why else would there be a full-size sailing ship over there in the distance, not to mention full-blown End Cities? Once you've explored the Outer Islands for a few minutes, you're bound to encounter some of these wacky structures, smothered in chorus plants and extending to great distances. Whether anyone is there to greet you or not will depend wholly on your single or multiplayer status, and whether they represent a threat is down to your chosen game mode. Best be cautious, though! You never know exactly who you're going to bump into around the corner.

WATCH OUT FOR SHULKERS!

So you walk into a chamber made of nice purpur blocks. You check the perimeter and secure the visible environment. All seems tranquil, so you settle down for a nice rest . . . Oh no you don't! Right above you, a shulker suddenly appears. This nasty mob, the third hostile native of the End after Endermen and the Ender Dragon himself, looks just like a normal purpur block, but will suddenly break in half. Inside the block there's an evil little face smiling out at you; it will then shoot guided missiles, that follow you wherever you go. Block or destroy these at all costs, or your stay down here in the End might well be cut short rather sooner than you predicted.

08

BATTLE THE ENDER DRAGON

To finally win through the End, you have a big job ahead of you — defeating the pesky Ender Dragon who has been circling in the sky and unleashing ender charges at you every time you get within a few blocks of it. Now it's time to teach this cheeky reptile who's boss around here, so grab your trusty bow and arrow — and let's rock! Deliver fatal damage to the dragon with carefully-aimed shots and it will gradually start to lose health. Watch out, though; the charges it shoots at you behave rather like potions of harming, with the advantage being that you can scoop them up into a bottle for later use as dragon's breath. While doing that, make sure it doesn't fly down and pulverize you, of course.

SMASH THE CRYSTALS

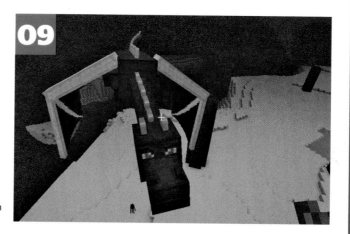

09

As you fight the Ender Dragon, keep a close eye on its behavior. It'll circle or strafe you, depending on your position, but occasionally it will also link via a white beam to a nearby ender crystal; it does this to recharge its health. Clearly this isn't ideal if you want to get the game finished before teatime, so make you sure you destroy the crystal while the recharging is happening and the dragon will take damage. If you need help isolating the right kill-points, use the F3+B shortcut to reveal the creature's eight surrounding hitboxes. Obviously any ranged weapons that you may have taken with you into a custom or modded environment will be a big help here. With a bit of determination, you'll end its reign of terror!

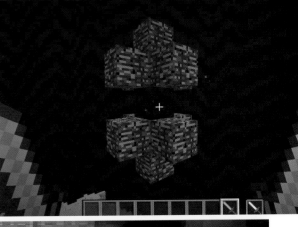

ENJOY THE ENDING

With ol' fiery-mouth dead as a doornail, you've conquered the End and completed your Minecraft mission! That's unless you want to resurrect the Ender Dragon for another battle (see below) or you're in a custom server or map where other adventures await you. Assuming said escapades are to be found up top in the Overworld, grab the dragon egg trophy dropped by the Ender Dragon and head for a gateway portal. On your way out you'll be saluted by the end poem, a few minutes' worth of conversation between two alien beings who wish to salute you on your progress and let you know some of the secrets of Minecraft's philosophy. If you want to skip this, you can — bigger and bolder adventures are waiting for you!

TIPS FOR THE END TIMES

Looking for quick tips for getting through the End in a mod-free Minecraft map? Look no further! You can get a lot done down here, whether it's eating cool food, having a try at the various hostile mobs of the End, or just getting from place to place, with no need to install one of those pesky mods . . .

Juicy fruit

1 Grab chorus fruit from chorus plants — it'll reduce your hunger and may give you an unexpected teleport ride!

Crystal clear

2 Want to fight the dragon again? Respawn it an unlimited number of times by laying four end crystals on the exit portal.

Beat your chest

3 Ender chests are like normal chests, except other players can't steal the contents. They have 27 storage slots, too.

Stone the crows

4 Use end stone for building structures; its blast resistance is 1.5 times that of normal stone, and the dragon can't destroy it.

Grab the pearl

5 Kill an Enderman and it may drop an ender pearl. Throw one and teleport to the spot where it lands!

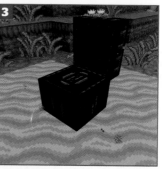

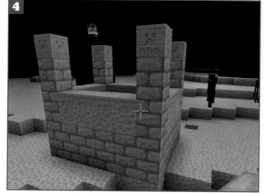

SURVIVORS' DIARY

SURVIVE AN ALIEN INVASION

Yes, the add-on's called Alien Invasion, but I wanted to see if you can befriend these extraterrestrials. Spoiler: It's not possible

eah, good one Mojang. So you release an Alien Invasion add-on for your Windows 10 and Pocket editions and expect **users to just kill all those** extraterrestrial visitors because that's what we've seen in movies (admittedly, all the best movies)? Well, you're **not pulling** the wool over my eyes, because I don't even have wool! Sure, I'm a dyed-in-the-wool free thinker, **but that's** just a special kind of **metaphorical wool that's been** dyed — and no little **green men** are dying on my watch. Where was I?

Oh yeah. I am heading into this add-on with my own objectives. **I will make friends** with these aliens. **I will show them that the true** heroes of Earth aren't the ones with diamond swords and the right Wiki page **open** to remember how to craft TNT — they're the ones with open arms, and a menu of alien-friendly food. These guys are going to love me.

HOUR 1
GET THE LOOK

Step 1: Choose the friendliest skin possible. I went with this one, wearing a manly apron and a big toothy grin. There's simply no way the aliens are going to mistake a face like that for that of a warmonger. There's a small chance they'll think I'm too friendly, and run away, but I'm willing to take that risk in the name of peace. So I guess I just stand under their ships and jump around to get their attention? It's the intergalactic dance of friendship - they'll be down here in a jiffy, and then I'll show them what Earth-TV and Earth-milk and Earth-gravel is like. Cannot. Wait.

HOUR 2
FIRST CONTACT

And would you look at that, this guy turned a corner and came running straight at me! He's an alien alright - he's got the green skin, the robot arms, the chittering sound effects, the surprisingly well-defined stomach muscles, the oh-so fashionable boots - he's everything you'd hope for from a space invader. Well, I say "he," maybe it's a girl. Or maybe there are no genders on the planet its from. Or a third gender, called "plob" or something! Man, I can't wait to ask him/her/plob all about alien culture. And it's so close now! Wait, why's he squaring up to punch me in the . . .

HOUR 4
BRUISED EGO

O kay, diary, that could have gone better. I got sucker-punched by a green punk. It's not been the ideal start to my interstellar peace process. No first contact should have to end with me punching the other person until they explode. Alas, I can only see two reasons for this outcome: 1) That alien had gone rogue - all his mates want to be chill with the humans, but he's just a bad'un. 2) I'm not dressed right. I'll just grab some armor, a load of old pork chops and some weaponry from these community chests, and see if they prefer my vibrant new style. Next stop - that spaceship up there.

HOUR 7
ENGINE TROUBLE?

I think I've solved the problem. The aliens weren't angry at me, it's just that their ships have broken down, and they're just angry in general. You know, like a dad when his SUV conks out ten miles from Center Parcs. I got up on top of the ship to find a door to get in and say hello, and instead I spotted these four big buttons, just jutting out of the roof. I've seen cars — if you want them to go, you need to push all the buttons in first. So I just need to prod these back into place, fix the ship, and make some friends from faraway in the process. Right, let's just stamp this one in.

HOUR 12

MECHANIC PANIC

O h good lord. Oh dear. Oh dearie me. I did not see that coming. I pushed the button in, and heard this sort of ominous clank. So I hopped back onto the skyscraper I climbed up, and ... and ... it just exploded. What idiot made these ships? I mean, there's loads of asteroids in space, one of them could easily hit the "explode immediately" button. It's just bad design. I really, really hope there was no one in there. There's no way they'll think I'm a cool guy if I just evaporated a couple of families.

HOUR 15

GUNGE PLUNGE

S o I just bumped into a load of sentient slime. They look nothing like the alien that socked me in the face earlier. A theory! These are intergalactic stowaways that slide into the cracks in alien spaceship hulls, hitching a ride all the way to a new planet, and gooping the whole place up. Now consider this: What if that wasn't an explosion button I pressed earlier, but a normal, non-explosion button that had just been gummed up by these slick critters? Well, that would mean I'd be doing my would-be alien mates a great favor by slicing them up as payback. Let's just draw the ol' sword ...

HOUR
18
CROWD CONTROL

Good news — I made short work of those slimes. Bad news — I get the feeling they were alien children or something, because a group of green guys saw me and have chased me up a wall. They look pretty miffed. I mean, it's fine - I didn't kill the slimes, they all just turned into two smaller slimes when I slashed them up. If anything, I gave them more children, so I don't really get the problem. I've been shouting "let's be friends" at this group for about 20 minutes now, and it doesn't really seem to be getting through to them. Wait a moment, what's that rumbling?

HOUR
20
THE BIG GUY

Setting aside the fact that I was too scared to realize I was inside a gigantic glass hall for a second, this is more like it. I'm pretty sure this guy's the boss, and he's come to greet me after all my shouting. About time. Now, how to communicate properly? Shouting and mechanical engineering haven't really worked so far, and those are my two real strengths. I guess I'll just go for a classic handshake and play it by ear if that goes well. Here goes, extending my arm. Oh wait. Oh no. I still have my sword equipped from the slimes earlier.

121

HOUR 21
A PLAN FOR MAN

Take a memo — accident or not, do not slash at the muscled leader of a technologically superior space-faring race with a little blue sword. I had to beat a pretty hasty escape from the hall there (well, he punched me through a window), and took shelter under a tree. Unfortunately so did this goon. Look at him, with his massive nose and his beige suit. Humans are so dull compared to aliens. I wouldn't have any trouble making cosmic chums if all these humans were just gone. Then I'd be the interesting one to the aliens instead of the other way around! Hmm. Wait a sec . . .

HOUR 22
PEW-MAN

I know this might seem like I've lost my mind in pursuit of an impossible (and some would say pointless) goal, but really I just call this advanced problem solving. What do you do when human civilization is stopping you from making new friends? You blow up a city with a cannon attached to a golden block. It's not supervillain-y, it's super-intelligent. It's extra lucky I brought this lever from home this morning — who's over-preparing now, mom? Let's just get that plugged in and get this city-leveling show on the road, shall we?

HOUR
23
MISFIRE

O kay diary, I need you to run some numbers for me. What are the odds that the aliens would have parked their mothership directly in front of a TNT cannon, and that alien metal is particularly susceptible to explosions. Also, that I didn't bother to check where it was pointing before I fired, and that the noise was much louder than I'd expected, leading me to wet myself a bit? I mean the odds on that must be just crazy. I am the unluckiest man in the world.

HOUR 24
NIGHT FRIGHT

T he aliens seem pretty angry with me. At least, I think that's what all that screaming was about — the optimist in me wants to say they're cheering because I got all their luggage down to ground level with the minimum of fuss, but I just don't buy it. I walled up the door just in case and sat on the roof as the sun went down. I'm starting to lose hope in my peace project. I mean, if wiping out your own species to make friends doesn't work, what will? Time to get some shut-eye. Hopefully something good will come up tomorrow.

HOUR 25
RUDE AWAKENING

This morning, I woke up with a jolt. Not because I'd dreamed up some inspiration — it was because a passing alien spaceship had fired some ball lightning into my spine and all my nerves went a bit crazy for a second. I thought better of lobbing some more TNT at it (I'm not a morning person, or an electricity-in-my-nervous-system person), and suddenly realized it wasn't passing at all. It was hovering above me, and firing its lightning toward a building across the city. It was pointing me there! I've TNT-ed my anti-alien wall down, and I'm about to set off to my destiny. I hope there are alien hugs involved in my destiny.